Harry and Walter

written by Kathy Stinson

illustrated by Qin Leng

annick press
toronto + berkeley + vancouver

We acknowledge the support of the Canada Council for the Arts, the Ontario Arts Council, and the participation of the Government of Canada/la participation du gouvernement du Canada for our publishing activities.

Cataloging in Publication

Stinson, Kathy, author
        Harry and Walter / Kathy Stinson ; Qin Leng, illustrator.

Issued in print and electronic formats.
ISBN 978-1-55451-802-9 (bound).—ISBN 978-1-55451-801-2 (paperback).—
ISBN 978-1-55451-803-6 (epub).—ISBN 978-1-55451-804-3 (pdf)

        I. Leng, Qin, illustrator II. Title.

PS8587.T56H37 2016   jC813'.54   C2015-905343-9
                                                           C2015-905344-7

Published in the U.S.A. by Annick Press (U.S.) Ltd.
Distributed in Canada by University of Toronto Press.
Distributed in the U.S.A. by Publishers Group West.

Printed in China

Visit us at: www.annickpress.com
Visit Kathy Stinson at: www.kathystinson.com

Also available in e-book format. Please visit www.annickpress.com/ebooks.html for more details.
Or scan

Dedicated to best friends Emmett and
Erling, whose story inspired this one.
—K.S.

To my Agong
—Q.L.

"Come on, Walter," Harry said. "Let's go."
Harry put his tractor in gear and off he went.
Walter put his tractor in gear and off he went.
"Wait up!" called Harry.

Harry was four and three-quarters. He had lived next door to Walter all his life. Walter was ninety-two and a half. He had lived in many places.

Side by side Harry and Walter zoomed across the grass between their houses. Harry said, "Vroooom! Vroooom!" "Heh, heh, heh," said Walter.

Sometimes Harry and Walter played games.

"Want to play croquet?" asked Walter.
"Okay," said Harry. "Which stick do you want?"
"Yellow," said Walter.
"Okay," said Harry. "I'll take the blue one."

Harry and Walter hit all the colored
balls through every hoop.

Then Harry said, "Walter, do your
tomato plants have tomatoes yet?"

"Let's go see."

Harry ran to Walter's garden.
"Tomatoes!" he shouted.
Catching up with Harry, Walter said,
"But they're still green."

When the tomatoes turned red, Harry and Walter each ate one—right there in Walter's garden. The juice dribbled down their chins.

When the leaves on the trees turned yellow and fell, Harry and Walter raked them into piles between their houses.

Harry and Walter did jigsaw puzzles and
played board games.
They drew pictures for each other—of tractors
and tomatoes and piles of leaves.
"You draw real good, Walter," said Harry.
Walter said, "You draw well too, Harry.
And if you keep at it, you'll get even better."

Harry showed Walter how to turn a car into a robot and march it across the floor.

Walter showed Harry how to turn a piece of paper into a bird and make it soar through the air.

"This is hard," said Harry. "I can't do it!"
"Keep trying," Walter said. "You'll get it. I know you will."

One day, when it wasn't too cold for young boys and old men, Harry and Walter made a snowman.

"Walter," Harry said, "you're my best friend."

"You're my best friend too, Harry."

"Let's be friends till I'm as old as you, okay?"

Walter rubbed his chin, thinking.
Then he said, "I'd like that, Harry. I'd like that very much."

When spring came all the snow melted and so did the snowman. Someone hammered a sign into the grass in front of Harry's house. *For Sale* the sign said.

Walter frowned and Harry cried. "I don't want to move!"

"Things change," Walter said. "I might have to move someday too."

The day the moving van came Harry and Walter
were so sad they couldn't even say good-bye.

Harry's new house had more grass than the old house.
Harry rode his tractor up and down between his house and
the house next door.
"Vroom," he said. "Vroom."
But riding without Walter wasn't much fun.

Harry's new house had a vegetable garden in the backyard.
But the tomatoes didn't taste as good as Walter's.

Harry's new house even had its own tree house.
One day when the leaves were starting to fall, Harry climbed the ladder, up, up, up.
Inside his tree house, he turned his car into a robot.

He turned pieces of paper into birds, just like Walter had shown him.
He flew his paper birds, one by one, out the window.
They fluttered like dead leaves to the ground.

But he kept trying to make a better bird.
Soon one of his birds did fly a little better than the others.
Still, Harry missed Walter so much.

He was about to toss out his last bird when . . .

"Walter!" Harry exclaimed. "What are you doing here?"

"I was taking a little walk when I saw your birds."

"All the way from your house to here?"

Walter pointed to an apartment building up the street.
"That's where I live now. It was time for me to move too."

Harry climbed down his ladder and hugged Walter so hard they almost fell over.

Walter laughed. "Like I said, Harry, things change."

"Yes, they do," Harry said. "I was four, and then I was five, and now I am six. Do you want to come and rake leaves with me?"

"I'm almost ninety-four," Walter said.
"Too old for raking leaves."
He leaned down and picked up two
perfect leaves, one red and one yellow.
"But there's something else we can do with
the leaves. Would you like me to show you?"

"I would like that, Walter. I would like that very much."

"Come on then, Harry. Let's go."

Harry took Walter's hand because some things don't change.
And off they went—the best of friends.